The Grand Bug Hotel

Flicker Finds Her Glow

Jodie Parachini

illustrated by Bryony Clarkson

Albert Whitman & Company
Chicago, Illinois

It's a very important day at The Grand Bug Hotel.
Today is Flicker's birthday.

It's a *wake up early, clean your antennas, shine your wings* day.

It's a *balloons and banners, cake and presents, games and parties* day.

But most importantly, it's a *find your GLOW* day.

Now that Flicker's not a baby bug anymore,
she's ready to discover her special something.

Something that sets her apart from all the other bugs.
Something that makes her one of a kind.
Something that makes her glow.

"Every bug has a special something," said Papa Jitterbug. "Something that makes us proud to be bugs!"

"It's what gives bees their buzz and ladybugs their spots and lightning bugs our glow!" said Mama Junebug.

Flicker was super-duper, extra-bugly excited.

"Soon I'll be able to flash and gleam and SHINE!"

But first Flicker had to find what made her special.

The twins tried to guess what would make Flicker glow.

"Is it that laughing makes you sneeze?" asked Flare.

"Or that you love honey ice cream?" said Zip.

Flicker laughed (and sneezed). "Every bug loves honey ice cream," she told the baby bugs, "so it can't be that!" But what *was* it?

Flicker wasn't sure. "Grampa Glowworm said I'll know when I know." But she still had so many questions.

What makes me special? and *How do I find it?*

"I know," Flicker said excitedly. "I'll ask my friends for help!"

Flicker's friends already had their special somethings.

Roly Poly had a strong but bendy shell.

"Look, Flicker! My shell is great for gymnastics!"

Boing! Bounce!

Maybe Flicker was a gymnast too. She leaped and rolled until her face was red.

"I don't think acrobatics is my special something." She sighed.

Roly Poly agreed.

Wicket loved making music.

He created beautiful sounds using his wings.

Chirp! Cheroouuup!

Flicker tried to make music too. She whistled and warbled and trilled. The others covered their ears.

"Maybe you're better at quiet things, Flicker," said Wicket kindly.

Dazzle was good at inventions.

"Look at this," she said.

Clang! Swish!

Maybe Flicker was an inventor too.

She tinkered and hammered until—**presto!**

Inventing certainly wasn't her special something.

"This is harder than I thought it would be," Flicker said. That gave her another idea. "Let's play dress up. I'm sure I'll find my special something that way."

They were superbugs
and swashbucklers
and sneaky
and curious.

"But none of these feels like ME!" said Flicker when they finished.

Then she had a terrible thought. "What if I'm the only bug without a special something? I'll never get my glow!"

"Does this mean there won't be a party?" asked Wicket.

"Or games?" asked Dazzle.

"Or cake!" moaned Roly Poly.

Flicker didn't know what else to do. Her wings drooped.

Flicker's friends gathered around her and gave her a big bug hug.

Flicker smiled. "I've got an idea," she said. "But I need your help."

The friends colored and cut and glued until it was all finished.

"Now it's time for a party!" Flicker announced.

"If I can't find *my* special something," said Flicker, "I'll make *everything around me* special."

"What a wonderful party," said Lord and Ladybug.

"We haven't played Pin the Tail on the Dragonfly in years," said Ant and Uncle.

Even Queen Bee was having fun.

When Mama Junebug finally dimmed the lights for cake, Grampa Glowworm winked and said, "Congratulations, Flicker, you found it!"

Flicker looked around. She didn't see anything different.

Grampa laughed. "Your ideas," he said. "They're always—"

"Cheerful!" said Roly Poly.

"Helpful!" said Wicket.

"Hopeful!" said Dazzle.

"And bright!" beamed Grampa Glowworm.

Flicker's cheeks flushed, and she felt warm all over.

She was...

GLOWING!
Happy birthday, Flicker!

Sophie, your "special something" is your amazing
imagination. This book is for you.—JP

For Finn, who shares Wicket's special something.—BC

Library of Congress Cataloging-in-Publication data
is on file with the publisher.
Text copyright © 2022 by Jodie Parachini
Illustrations copyright © 2022 by Albert Whitman & Company
Illustrations by Bryony Clarkson
First published in the United States of America in 2022
by Albert Whitman & Company
ISBN 978-0-8075-2508-1 (hardcover)
ISBN 978-0-8075-2510-4 (ebook)
Printed in China
10 9 8 7 6 5 4 3 2 1 WKT 26 25 24 23 22 21

Design by Rick DeMonico

For more information about Albert Whitman & Company,
visit our website at www.albertwhitman.com.